the GRUMP

Written and Illustrated by

Mark Ludy

GPPI

Green Pastures Publishing, Inc.
Longmont, Colorado

A dog started to bark and then another and another. Joining in the chorus were children rushing through the streets, yelling, "He's coming! He's coming!" People did not need to ask, "Who's coming?" They knew well who it was. Every Thursday this warning sounded, and when it did, all work halted and the streets cleared. A dog's yelp could be heard, and people knew his cane had found its mark. As he drew closer, they heard the tapping of his cane upon the cobblestones, which signaled each approaching step.

Then suddenly the figure came into view: an old man dressed in rich finery, a tall silk hat covering straggly white hair. A scowl etched itself deeply into his face. The very sight of him made people tremble. They knew his spiteful glare. They knew his temper. And everyone knew his name — Mr. McCurry Brogan Howlweister, more commonly referred to as the Grump.

❀

The small but lively village of Dinkerwink had been settled hundreds of years before this day. Most of the families could trace their roots to Dinkerwink's beginnings, so of course they knew one another well. Dinkerwinkians were a people of unique talents and quirks and oddities, of all shapes and smells and shoe sizes. Miss Paddlewack, a most generous lady, was well known for her horrific apple pies. Her generosity spread pies throughout the homes of Dinkerwink, and because most Dinkerwinkians tried to be polite, they received her gifts with smiles and thanks. Mr. Brunko, a funny and charming man, simply had to wear the same pair of socks every Thursday. Just by looking at Mr. Brunko's ankles, Dinkerwinkians knew for certain that it was Thursday, the day the Grump would come to town. Sweet, plump Mrs. Millenberry was a favorite of the children, for she gave them luscious peaches-and-cream suckers. They didn't mind that she had a laugh that shrilled and squeaked, wheezed and whined. Despite their differences, the people of Dinkerwink were friendly and liked one another ... but no one liked Mr. McCurry Brogan Howlweister.

❀

In the village of Dinkerwink, no one exchanged words with Mr. McCurry Brogan Howlweister except Marcel, the grocer. Once a week the Grump hobbled into town and entered the grocer's humble shop. As was his custom since the days Marcel's grandfather had been the grocer, he would go first to a rack of freshly baked bread and help himself to a few loaves. Then he would choose a round of cheese and a bottle of wine and make his way to the counter. Marcel would greet him with a faltering voice, "Thank you, Mr. Howlweister, for doing business with us." Shyly he would take the coins from the Grump's outstretched hand. Before going his way, the Grump would peer into the distracting face of a little girl who sat on a stool next to the counter. She had the sweetest of smiles, and seeing that smile, the Grump would grunt disagreeably.

❀

This particular Thursday, the Grump performed his usual business, bought his usual groceries, grunted his usual response to the child, and departed from the grocer's shop. It was customary for him to take his time in leaving town, for he rather enjoyed the wide-eyed stares of the people and the ill effect his presence had on them. It pleased him to send one more annoying dog sprawling under the wrath of his cane. Numerous times the villagers had seen him whack a young lad's ankle if the boy approached him on a dare.

A short distance from town and on the far side of Wallaco Woods was his home, a dark and fearful walk for any but the Grump. The mansion atop a hill was guarded by a tall iron fence, the only entrance a rickety gate of swirls and spikes. Aged stonework and gargoyles gave the mansion a haunting appearance.

Entering his home, the Grump lit a candle and carried it through rooms of costly furniture which lay beneath white sheets, protected but never enjoyed. The house creaked and moaned, longing for breath in the staleness. He climbed the winding stairway to an enormous room. He lit a fire in the grate, then lit his pipe and sat until the fire went cold. As he did every evening, the Grump put on his nightgown, set his slippers and cane beside the bedstand, and went to bed, staring at the ceiling as he drifted to sleep. He was alone and that was how it had always been.

Suddenly his eyes opened. A knocking echoed through the empty corridors of the house. Was someone at his door? No visitor had lifted the knocker of that door for years. The Grump rose from his bed and slid into his slippers. He set flame to the candle, then hobbled through the hallway, down the winding stairway and through the dark rooms to the front door. "Who goes there? Name yourself!" There was no answer. Again he cried, "Who's there?" and waited for a response, but none came.

Laying the candle aside, he lifted the latch and threw open the door. Moonlight and the freshness of night air flooded the entry. The Grump stepped onto the porch, quite ready to give the trespasser a thrashing with his cane, but the perpetrator of this night's rude awakening was nowhere to be seen. Angrily, the Grump shouted, "And don't come back!"

He turned toward the door and then stopped, his eyes drawn to an object near his feet. It was a crudely wrapped and ribboned package. The Grump bent and drew the package into his hands. He twisted it and turned it, shook it and stared at it. Then with one last glance around, he went inside. He secured the door and hurriedly removed the wrapping. A confounded look crossed his face as he held before him neatly cut out paper people, all connected and folded like an accordion. Thinking the gift a rude joke, he took it in both hands, crumpled it, and tossed it into a dark corner of the room.

❀

The people of Dinkerwink, it is true, shared common feelings about the Grump and often gossiped about him. Dinkerwinkians taught their children the importance of loving their neighbors and forgiving others as they themselves had been forgiven. Yet there was one exception—Mr. McCurry Brogan Howlweister. Who could love this mean and inconsiderate man? This had been the thinking for as long as anyone could remember.

But then a child had been born in Dinkerwink, a child who would be different from the rest. She was Lydia, daughter of Marcel, the grocer, and his wife Tamilia. As Lydia had grown, people had thought her an unfortunate child, for little Lydia could neither hear nor speak. They often whispered about her to one another, "Poor child, what a pity, what a pity!" But Lydia's adoring parents loved her. She was their only child, their precious gift.

Lydia was a beautiful child. She had full brown hair and large, dark eyes. Her face was sprinkled with tender little freckles. Adorable and completely huggable she was, a picture of innocence. Marcel and Tamilia often showered her with loving words, but knowing she could not hear their voices, they held her tightly to show her how precious she was. Lydia's most treasured possession was her rag doll Jewell, a gift from her beloved father. She had loved the stuffing right out of her friend and dear companion. Lydia knew the sweetness of love.

Lydia did not play with other children but was not lonely. The streets and homes of Dinkerwink were her familiar friends, and the countryside beyond was a world of pure delight. Often, with Jewell on her lap, she would sit amid the flowers of the fields, pretending to be their special guest for mid-morning tea. Every afternoon she sat on her stool beside the counter in her parents' shop and smiled at those who came to buy. All took blessing from that smile—all but the Grump.

A week had passed since the appearance of the package, and the Grump made his Thursday journey into town. This day he seemed even grumpier than normal, evidenced by a repertoire of growls, grunts and other awful noises more frightening than usual. He entered Marcel's shop, the familiar scowl upon his face. So out of sorts was he that he didn't think to pick up his cheese, and when he saw the smile of that little girl, he became extremely vexed, threw his coins on the counter and left the shop with haste.

At home beside a comfortable fire, the Grump calmed himself. He sat in his chair, dozing, until the fire died, then rose to go to bed. Immediately, he was jarred by a knock that resounded through the house. This time he would not give the trespasser an opportunity to run. He hurried through the house as fast as his old legs would allow and, flinging open the door, shouted, "Who goes there?" He looked to his right and he looked to his left. He could find no one. Perhaps, he thought, a ghost was haunting him, but he dismissed the thought as he observed a shadowy figure running into Wallace Woods. "Hooligan," he muttered to himself.

On the porch lay another gift, wrapped and tied with ribbon as before. Wincing and wheezing, he picked it up, this time in a hostile manner, as a sign to any who might secretly look on that he was not impressed. He went inside.

As he unfolded the wrapping, he was startled to find a large heart made from colorful paper. It was decorated in a childlike way, with a smiling face in the center. He could not understand. He did not want to understand. He crushed and tossed the heart into the dark corner with the paper people and went to his room, disgusted.

Had the Grump better eyesight, he would have seen that the mysterious figure vanishing into the woods was none other than a child, her mound of hair bobbing up and down and a glow encircling her so radiantly that the forest itself might have thought it was daybreak. She skipped through Wallaco Woods and into town.

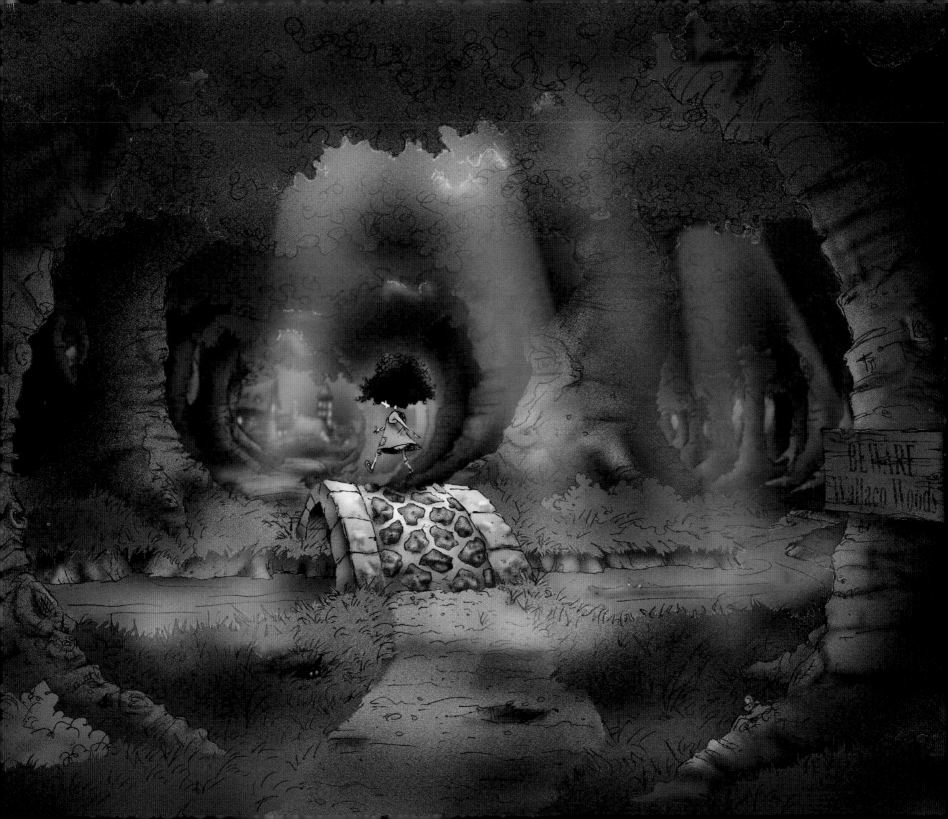

From street to street she skipped, and reaching the open window of her bedroom,
crawled up and in. Lifting the sheet, the child snuggled into her bed and wrapped
her arms around the love-worn doll and in a moment was asleep.

Another week passed, and the Grump made his way to Marcel's shop. His face looked ragged and tired. He had spent most of his nights awake in his chair, pipe in hand, unable to sleep. Marcel's eyes greeted those of the Grump and found them glaring at him. Marcel looked away. Then feeling a sense of duty, he lifted his eyes and said, "Welcome, Mr. Howlweister." The Grump not only ignored the grocer's pleasantries but was unusually hostile as he paid for his purchases. Turning to leave, he looked straight at the child on the stool and into her sweet smile. How that smile disturbed him!

The Grump was troubled and confused. Who had visited him, and why had this person left worthless gifts upon his porch? As he walked home through Wallaco Woods, he formed a plan that would help him to discover who the scoundrel was.

❀

At sunset, he hid near the porch behind a row of lilac bushes. The Grump was quite prepared to wait—and wait he did. He struggled to stay alert. His eyelids fluttered, his thoughts drifted, and old memories, unhappy and unwelcome, flooded his mind.

As far back as he could remember, the people of Dinkerwink had kept their distance from him. His own father had been distant, traveling to faraway places to make his fortune. Young McCurry Brogan Howlweister had never known his mother, for she had died when he was born. He had been left in the care of a guardian, a harsh elderly woman who had kept tight rein upon the boy, never allowing him the company of other children and taking him from the mansion only to make their weekly visit to the grocer's shop. Games and fun, gifts and toys were not part of young McCurry's childhood. His days were nothing but drudgery, strict discipline, and endless hours of loneliness. He had thought these memories were long forgotten, but now he remembered.

The sound of footsteps startled him. He listened closely, clenching the end of his cane, prepared to give this intruder of the night an unforgettable fright. He chuckled quietly as he imagined the surprise upon that scoundrel's face. "You'll pay," he whispered as the figure approached, its lengthy shadow playing upon the grass in the moonlight. "You'll pay."

Like a cat on the prowl, he slowly made his way around the bush. His heart beat wildly. With cane raised high, he cried out, "Who goes there? Name yourself!"

In the brightness of the moon, he saw her on the porch. He watched, quieted now by curiosity. She did not answer, for she could not hear his demand, loud and angry though it had been. With her back to the Grump, she placed a package on the porch, then lifted and dropped the knocker at the door and turned to leave. She stopped abruptly; her eyes grew wide. Before her was the man for whom her gift was intended.

They stood face to face, not moving, not blinking. This was the girl who sat by the grocer's counter. This was the mysterious one who had caused the Grump his sleepless nights.

The girl caught her breath and, reaching down, picked up the package. She held out her gift to the Grump and smiled. The Grump looked at the gift and then at Lydia.

He took the gift. For a long, quiet moment he held it, then loosened the ribbon and opened the wrapping. His face reddened and his mouth twitched. His eyes squinted and his body squirmed. No one in Dinkerwink would have believed what happened next.

Mr. McCurry Brogan Howlweister's eyes brimmed with tears and he began to tremble. His legs gave way, and he collapsed on the steps and cried ... and cried ... and cried.

On the front steps of the mansion upon the hill sat a man whose cold heart had been pierced by the gift of love, a little girl by his side patiently comforting him.

❀

Thursday came and Thursday passed. Mr. Brunko had worn his Thursday socks. Dinkerwinkians had done their Thursday work. Children had played their usual games. But the dogs hadn't barked and the children hadn't yelled, "He's coming!" Marcel had kept his shop open, waiting until the sun had set and the snores of the neighbors could be heard through the open windows, until it was clear the Grump was not coming.

Dinkerwink was not prepared. The Grump was disrupting their normal routine. The next day they waited expectantly, thinking he would come and that life as usual could resume. But he did not come.

One of the oddest days in Dinkerwinkian history began as an ordinary Wednesday, with dogs wandering, children playing, shopkeepers doing business, and Mr. Brunko wearing ordinary socks. Miss Paddlewack was crossing the street to deliver one of her apple pies. Admiring the pie in her hands, she was not attentive to where she was going and quite unexpectedly bumped into someone.

"Oh, my! I'm so sorry! I was just delivering this delicious apple pie to …." Her words trailed into a gasp. The pie dropped from her hands and fell topside down into the street. Shrieking, she ran.

All around, Dinkerwinkians looked up from what they were doing. A wave of silence swept the villagers as they watched the familiar figure walk around the toppled pie and continue on, cane tapping upon the cobblestones. The dogs were strangely quiet.

Marcel was stocking the shelves when he heard the jingling of the bell above his door. Without turning around, he welcomed his customer, "Good day to you!" Moving through the shop, the man selected his items and brought them to the counter. Aware that his customer was waiting, Marcel came around, wiping his hands on a towel then laying it aside. "Will this be all for you today?" As Marcel looked up, he was visibly startled. "Mr. Howlweister! I didn't know it was you!" For a moment the Grump looked at Marcel, then gave him a handful of coins for the purchase. "Thank you, Mr. Howlweister, for doing business with us."

To Marcel's surprise, as well as that of the people of Dinkerwink, whose noses, ears, and fingers were pressed in curiosity to the store's windows, the Grump spoke ... and what a strange utterance it was! "No, I thank *you.*"

Then he turned toward the little girl sitting on her stool next to the counter. Putting his hand inside his coat, he drew out a box wrapped in plain paper and placed it upon her lap. She looked at the box and then at him, and her eyes asked the question, "Is this for me?" He nodded, and as he did so, the Grump's mouth relaxed ... and he smiled.

Lydia removed the wrapping and carefully lifted the lid of the box. Oh, what joy! On a bed of lilacs lay a flower doll, its dress of pink hollyhocks, its hat a small wild sunflower. It wore a necklace of white clover woven into a circlet. Lydia gently lifted the doll from the box and held it to her heart, rocking from side to side. The Grump looked on, tears spilling, then turned to leave.

Lydia placed the doll on its bed of blossoms and slid down from the stool. Before the Grump could reach the door, she slipped her small hand into his, and together they walked into the brightness of the day, into a crowd of stunned Dinkerwinkians. With the dearest of smiles, she hugged the man known as the Grump, and he, with newfound tenderness, touched the ringlets of her hair.

Then joy flooded Dinkerwink and there was happy celebration. There was laughter, there was fun ... and there was forgiveness. Mrs. Millenberry couldn't contain herself and passed out peaches-and-cream lollipops to everyone. Mr. Brunko declared this Wednesday to be a holiday in honor of Mr. McCurry Brogan Howlweister and went home to get his Thursday socks. Miss Paddlewack vowed that her next apple pie would be for the man who was no longer grumpy.

Mr. McCurry Brogan Howlweister felt warmth inside that he had never known. In the people's faces he saw a genuine kindness toward him, something new and inviting, something that made his smile feel right. It was like an embrace, strong and caring—a hug from all of Dinkerwink.

It was the heart of a little girl that had made the difference, the girl who now held the Grump by the hand. She was the only one in all of Dinkerwink who did not know Mr. McCurry Brogan Howlweister by that name. To Lydia he had just been the man with the upside down smile, a man who needed a friend to turn it right side up.

This book is dedicated to the sweet orphan child Lydia, whom I met only once, but that meeting changed my life forever.

Mark and Lydia
Bulgaria 1992

My Lord, I thank you for giving me a hope, a purpose and a love for people. You have made all this possible.

Paul and Sue Farabaugh, from the outset you have been there. You have stuck it out with me and I am thankful for your lives.

Pat Brunner, you shine! For the labor of love you've poured into editing this book and for encouraging my life, I will be forever grateful.

Ellen Edwards and Debra Garretson, much thanks ... I appreciate you.

Coffee shops in the Boulder County region, I thank you for offering me cheap office space and good friendships.

My family ... ever refreshing and full of love. Each one of you is a wonder and delight.

I am so thankful for friends. Your support and encouragement have kept me going.

My Woveydovey, I'm still waiting patiently ... I love ya!

Photo by Dwyer Photography
Longmont, Colorado

First Printing

Design and Layout by Mark Ludy and Ellen Edwards
Edited by Pat Brunner and Debra Garretson

Green Pastures Publishing, Inc.
Box 1808
Longmont, Colorado 80502
303.684.9118
Book Orders: 888.871.8694
Email: paul@greenpastures.com
Website: www.greenpastures.com

Publisher's Cataloging-in-Publication
(Provided by Quality Books, Inc.)

Ludy, Mark.

The Grump / written and Illustrated by Mark Ludy. -- 1st ed.
p. cm.
SUMMARY : Grumpy Mr. Howlweister, a feared legend in the town of Dinkerwink, has his heart changed by the compassion and love of a little girl.
LCCN : 00-190056
ISBN : 0-9664276-1-0

1. Deaf children -- Juvenile fiction. 2. Caring -- Juvenile fiction.
I. Title

PZ7.L9763Gr 2000   [Fic]
QB100-223

Printed in S. Kore